CH00920086

THE ACCUMUL,
SMALL ACTS OF

THE ACCUMULATION OF SMALL ACTS OF KINDNESS

Selima Hill

Chatto & Windus
LONDON

Published in 1989 by
Chatto & Windus Ltd
30 Bedford Square
London W C I B 3 S G

A C I P catalogue record for this book
is available from the British Library.

I S B N 0 7011 3455 0

Photoset by Rowland Phototypesetting Ltd
Bury St Edmunds, Suffolk
Printed in Great Britain by
Redwood Burn Ltd
Trowbridge, Wilts

Contents

Note to Reader

Italics are used for the imaginary voices the diarist hears in her head; double quotation marks for the direct speech of doctors, visitors, etc.; and single quotation marks for indirect speech or words she reads or remembers reading.

PART ONE
The In-Patient

CHAPTER 1 Boys

Whatever's the point of writing it all in code?
Supposing the coat is a monk,
and the sofa's a young horse;
and supposing the photos are real?
Darling, I love you.

I want to stay here in the dark for ever.
Everyone, don't talk and move around.

'A strange lamented artist who loves dancing.'
Somebody's clock. I hate her. Cold white lines.
Cut light in concave triangles, the door,
the side of the door, the panel's lonely back.
I think I am a sponge. I think I'm going.
Or shall I write in code again? Who cares.

She was descending like a boneless swan.
I wish more people would descend like that.
She knows I'm writing about her. Now she's gone.
Mr. C. is calling. Here I am,
hidden in my wooden hold of doors.
Last night G. told me everything. It's true:
I will always remember you, G., I really will.
I wanted to tell you about . . . I nearly did.

She asked me if I masturbate. Wet grass.
Hepburn – 'fragile, feminine' – please die.
Rays of light returning on themselves.
Glossy prints of Rudolf Nureyev.

Taut purity of virgins in white landscapes,
overwhelmed by tenderness.
Don't go.
"Like drugs," he said, "the same basic principle."
'Rebellion itself's a form of love.'

Obsession with counting birds.
My lips are aching.

They have taken away my Lord.
The Head is calling.

Marine crustaceans' seven leg-like mouths.
Goodwin's MOODS AND TENSES. Pipe tobacco.
'Little did the author know.'
Plisetskaya.
I wonder if I'm good at telling lies.
'Un homme secret, il danse dans la rue.'
I do not know the rules.
Oh yes you do!

"What's she really like?"
She is a virgin.
Yellow parrots, lettuce, nylon wool.
I went back to the study after supper.
The bluebells are in session in the woods.
Wearing dresses frightens me.
Calves.
Nipples.
The teachers smell of beans and dressing-gowns.

The dark proud gentleness of feathers
reflected in the dancer's famous face.
Her hair is gold. She hates the other partner.
Black satin, tinsel, armaments unfold.
She didn't know she made me cry. I told her.
Broad hands. Dark blood. A little milk and rice.
Down down down to the creator
of diamonds and coal and roots in silver tights.
Beaten cut tormented killed and counter-killed.
This isn't what you think. It's radioactive.
Many men and unknown things go down there.
Won't write about the walk. Past. Frozen colour.

Noises echo through the whitened squares.
'Mauriac choisit Emmanuelle.'
Hiding during meals – the seventh day.
I won't be watched so much by people later.

'Slowness Is Beauty' – always at top speed.
"I simply came to see if you're alright . . ."
'Suppressed depression, iron will' – that's me!
"You'll burn your journal next year – DEFINITELY."
Her fatherland. Tormented hope. Horned tree.

'Albert Schweitzer – famous bearded saint,
authority on Goethe and musician.'
'A policeman drags away a limp protester.'
'It is difficult to assess how far the jazzman
"sends" himself in the course of any session.'
The best thing they could do is to invent
a nice white dye that they could dye us with.
'Early evening in Trafalgar Square –
police begin their long removal job.'
MYSTERY MAGAZINE. I want a letter.
Writing a list of the people I have kissed – no,
writing a list of the people who've kissed me.

I have not been in Hall for eighteen days.
Chicken, peaches, cheese.
I don't know why.
'Some of the young Germans taking part
rebuild the vestries of the old cathedral.'
I want to go to B. The grass is shining.
Why do I write his name? It isn't true.
I threw the chocolate biscuits in the bushes.
Everyone is eating.
G.'s in tears.
It is not *God* who must be good and kind.
Patients eat in teams.
The rivers wind.

My socks are blood-soaked.
Gradual shapeless gloom.
I've dreamt of it three times.
White grapes for supper.
I took them all outside.

Nobody saw.
Running when exams are over.
Paris.
I'm going to eat outside again tonight.
Frosted hay. The smell of chives and boots.
I will be sixteen in the night.
My poetry.
I want to wash my hair.
I think she's looking.

H. has got a photo. I will steal.
It's all because of H. I told you so.
Everything she's got I want.
I'll scream.

Copulation in the form of memories.
Attempts in parents' bedroom.
Cockle-shells.
'Sensible comme les bouchers.'
Banded snails.
Boys in leather jackets wait for girls.
I want it. Knees like huts. *I want it, I want it.*
The Bishop of Wool. His gracious reality. Nuts.

"This doubling back she mentions seems to be
the most dynamic and influential sensation":
the door is for a long moment opened –
the timeless curling motion – sand and toes . . .
All I can write is *Love me, love me, love me.*
The unforgettable dream. The golden sand.
The unforgettable dream, already forgotten.
All I can write is gathered in my hand.

He was kissing a different woman every time.
I don't know how to laugh. *Hilarious laughter.*
'Dans le petit berceau peint en blanc,
il attendra le retour de Belmondo.'
Still telling me I write too much. I know.
'Who saw in death love's dark immaculate flower.'

They don't warm slippers. Painted houses. Grass.
I don't know where I'm going. Frothy water.
The sound of pouring coal and barking spaniels.
'*Et sur vos lèvres meurent les Caratines.*'

Cows sitting down.
White sugar.
Being in love.
And when one starling leaves,
they all fall over.
The road, the frost, the pram, the spinning spokes.
Two sumptuous new creations drench my body.
Headmistresses adjust their iron gates.
Tearing out the bits about themselves.
The tired Indian waiters slip in snow.
"She calls my girl-friends 'lodgers'."
Concubines!
Words like cats.
Compulsion to repeat.
I smell delicious.
Swimming. Feel my skin.
It is confined to small remoter pools.
'Artists lie most when they tell the truth.'
'A way of life commensurate with their beauty.'
'*Sie lebten mit ihrer Mutter in einer Sandgrube.*'

She was actually giving away the man she loved.
The letter had been opened. Full of pictures.
The road was blocked. They told us to use ladders
specially painted for us by the nurses.
We had to walk through lighted farm buildings.
I don't mean any harm.
My eyes are open.

The bus-conductor says I'm looking kinky.
The poet is God's spy, his velvet cushion.
'. . . and if not Love, then a very strong desire
to see you RIGHT HERE NOW!'

Cake, golden syrup.
Shouting at the pool.
Don't try to come.
Music pursuing something.
Breaking glass.
Hope D. won't try to come.
It's all gone wrong.
His apartment, his trousers, his books,
his nutmeg smell.

She says why don't I ever brush my hair.

One of my most likely days. Hot weather.
DOMINI EST TERRA 24
Being pregnant makes me feel dishonest.
Now I sleep with foreign men in dreams.
My hand froze on her neck, the dancer said.
Sigmund Freud, I know you can see my knickers.

Long hot babies sleep in ticking taxis.
Compulsive rhyming.
Please don't start again.
Talking in bed. The tranquil bay. The ponies.
Her pale breasts like fish. "No, she's not here."
Pulverous or ductile; not metallic.
Totality of perfect rest.
Afraid.

Ginger ale, paddling, menstruation.
No one but my foe to be my guide.
Hampstead in the autumn, lost for ever.
Wash face, clap hands, cut paper, telephone.
Lie around, read letters, think of sex.
It's snowing and she's cut her perfect hair.
And feared his hopes and hers and all were perished.
He thought about me when I was away.
Virginity – a hive of honey bees.
Four-minute warning.
Pleats.

His sticky fingers.
The blankets are our summer . '. . . *As ful ofté*
Next the foulé netlé, rough and thikké,
The rose waxeth souté and smothé and softé . . .'

The little ring, the little ruthless lover
who let himself in through the rosy door.
Being good in bed.
Lost by the river.
'Attach yourself to beings, not ideas.'
Hens engender warm simple relationships.
"Your hair-style – what do you call it?"
Mystic grace.

'All your hopes are substitutes for sorrow.'
Distant mountain animals lie dead.
D. is ringing soon. What did I feel like?
He ate his soup in silence like a barge.
Sitting on the steps of the Corn Exchange,
their handbags on their knees.
I think I'm bleeding.

Both the cats are miaouing. We won't feed them.
We think it's much more fun than being kind.
A man in a suit is waving from a sports car.
If only my hair was straight.
The sun is blind.

Exaggeration of physical contact in public.
But what is the point of saving time? she said.
Training a flea. 'Nehru is dead.' Eternity.
"You know your mother thinks you're very ill."
Daddy-long-legs, alder flies, small wasps;
the undulating membrane; we inhale.
Mogadon-entranced, the loving comes.
Chi-chi adores collapsing. Shut the door.

Night positions not so bad. The field.
So this is what it's like!

Our being grounded.
I'm going to be so calm. Christ. Tell the doctor.
I'll catalogue it truly if I do.
Address is very long. What shall I wear?
The grey-green twilight infiltrates my hair.
O Mother, O Mother, provider of comfortable jerseys,
I feel the cold night air ascend the lawn.

CHAPTER 2 Sons

Eight babies have been brutally attacked.
The day I saw the nurse, her cheek was bleeding.
His hair was very dark when he was born.
Orange tulips polished by the midwife.
It's silly to be frightened. Look, it's cosy.
He wore his little bonnet which I hated.
She knows when they are crying 'for attention'.
I thought I loved him more than all the rest.

She comes indoors and tidies up his toys.
She puts his cockatoo beside his chair.
She plays him music while he's in his bath.
She told me not to leave him, but I did.
I am the Mother from the Baby Ward.
He's screaming for the breast from which he's torn.

Trixie loves sweet tea.
She rides big horses.
She thinks the ballet dancer's really nice.
The circulating phosphorescent nurses,
stubbing out her endless cigarettes,
whisper things I promise not to tell her.
Trixie darling, rolled in wincyette.

When her daughter left, she kissed the window.
Mary, Mary, go to Intensive Care.
Women walk in different ways with baskets.
One of them's my mother. *Please don't laugh.*
Freshly washed, injected by the nurses,
I fold my lemon candlewick. Goodbye.
She waited for me patiently in VISITORS.
Seven years they said she waited there.

My breasts are rocks of milk.
They found the razor.
The orange flowers kicked the jug again.
Repeated fish are cruising round the curtains.

The giraffes are really nuns.
"She's so fucked-up!"

He fell out of his angulated buggy
watching polar bears, the doctor said.
Walled birds, caged gardens, ox-blood leather buttons;
a box of glass; a little one-armed mother.
At the clinic queuing for injections,
I can feel my occupant's soft limbs.

There's the rabbit, there's the coat I knitted him.
My breasts hang down and brush his lips like pears.
The Sister says I don't look like a mother.
Every day I hear his little prayers.

Little cubes of bread and peanut-butter.
He keeps on falling off the bed.
Don't cry.
There is a tiny boy sleeps next to mine
who was seven inches long when he was born.
He's lying underneath his yellow teddy;
he never lets it go; he never smiles.

We like it here. It's cool. I stroke my nightie.
We're going to eat our ices at the zoo.
My socks are blood-soaked but it doesn't matter.
The night nurse is a little baby too.

Sitting in the day-room with his wife,
he even finds the daffodils too 'physical'.
The babies smell of custard tarts.
Deep breathing.
I thought she was being angry so I cried.
I must steal Mary's milk in the morning.
The after-coming head.
Collapsing wives.
The nurse came in to make my bed. She's knackered!
Milk and blood will cloud the tepid bath.
Fluffy babies make their mothers love them,

fast asleep with prune-juice in their hair.

The gorilla's house is dark.
He wants his biscuits.
He seems to hover on the verge of tears.
We never feel cold.
We are the mothers.
Found at last, her baby on her knee.

I told him not to hit her but he did.
Who is that little boat for?
Not for me.
Beetroot. Boiled egg. A bowl of custard.
Elephants.
THE SEA OF GALILEE.

I stopped the car, and saw it was a baby.
At first I thought it was a little dog.
I wrapped it in a coat and brought it over.
"He ought to be much quieter, oughtn't he?"

Pastilles in a tin.
A bunch of keys.
Wipe away his tears,
his Pyrenees.

The children are asleep like little bags,
the tulips are as sweet as marzipan,
the cabbages are blue,
the house-boat's red.
The shaggy dog, once so devoted, 's dead.

The sound of heavy boots on the gravel.
It would have been unbearable, I know.
Smoking rollies on the day-room roof-top.
"The first thing that she did was bite the nurse."
I must assume a normal public face.
"She's been here since July."
My eyelids close.
Once D. came in and saw the new day breaking.

My uterus felt like a sunlit knife.
He's got a nice big face, I don't know why.
He doesn't smell like us, but of potatoes.

He's like a plum fished out of milky custard.
Endless cries of birds.
The sound of hoeing.

A bag of figs, a jug of milk, a shawl.
Full of roses.
"Shall we all go swimming?"
A field full of hares, worn smooth by cows.
They shake their soft square heads.
A little lull.
Pounding down the beach into the sea,
his fragile head was broken.
It's unkind.
'You've got to go on crying all your life.'
I thought you would look after him for me.

Wherever a child is born, a woman is wasted.
We do not quite belong to ourselves.
Always happy in the swimming-pool,
I manage to escape into my square.
Mixing cabbage salad with their fingers;
running towards me with their arms outstretched,
crushing all the hollyhocks with teddies,
the wa-wa babies stumble: "Lift me up!"

You see, it is so lonely I get serious.
Dream of a dream and shadow of a shade.
'The writer's instinct is essentially heartless.'
The wa-wa babies burst into floods of tears.

Cherry nougat for the quiet children.
Fond memories –
milk jelly,
sunny weather.
It's far away, and they don't notice it,

or if they do, they don't tell anyone.

The doctor says she's terrified of cats.
A jar of bluebells
tremble in the window.
"I know what people think –
some terrible things!"

She ran away and lived on bread and chocolate
hidden in the bottom of her pram.

Miles away from anywhere,
like fish.
I want to see a doctor.
I'm in bed.
The boy is tired but happy in the moonlight.
I saw some, falling faster, stuck with blood.
I sleep curled up like shrimps in the darkness.
I long for scenes where man has never trod.
A less soft but a straighter whiteness rises.
Mother Water, I'm your baby now.
A bedside light emits a stream of questions.
Do not console me. I am not your friend.
The yellow flip-flap of the albatross.
Now snow is filling up my little head.

Like a butcher, deep in rubber buckets,
tearing the hearts from cows' defrosting blood.
Stuck in one position like a statue.
You never lift a finger.
Sunlit bone.
Illuminated gloves. They killed my kitten.
He was the shyest man I ever met.
I wish I was a nice friendly person.
I wonder why he's dirty.
Let's go home.

My father used to sleep in the stables.
My mother knew at once when I made love.
The man who is a bird smokes No. 6's.
"Put your empty packet in the bin."
The nipples floating in the soup are carrots.
My father's got a hornet on his chin.

Far out, the lonely golfers start to cry.

The anorexic suffocates in chocolate.

My father wears a woolly cardigan
with lozenges of fear inside the pocket.

Seafarers gently drift across the ocean
with dogs and chickens in their long canoes
and colonize the islands east of China.

He said it was his wedding. It's not true.

I thought you'd be so pleased –
I shot the rabbits!
Strips of striped pyjamas soaked in tea.
The bulldog's blood drips on the red linoleum.
Her fingernails jump about like fleas.
I think they are thinking of Anna,
washing cherries.
He thought he was a goose.
I'm not surprised!
The driver's going so fast they'll all get flattened.
Beaded whisks of tails to swat fat flies.

Lying on the kitchen floor to hug him.
The doctor should be here any minute.
The yellow parrot saying *What a pity*.
Now his watch is ticking in my ear.
It's true he was my lover. *What a pity*.
The sun needs hearts of warm blood every day.
We're old enough to sleep here in fine weather.
Gertrude Bell has linen-covered thighs.
Jealous of the hands that touched the breasts
he was the first to marvel at. *Don't worry*.
So easily you'd think he's used to it.
The light that fills the world sleeps in my bed.
Waking up from dreams of frozen valleys
and violet bluebells nodding by the pools.
The face of God the doctor said I touched.
And loneliness in pink kneels down to pray.
The bedrooms house a family of camels.
"I hate to see a coffee getting cold."

The doctors say I read too much.
They're staring.
Her mouth is stuffed with custard-yellow wool.

He always hates the girls that he has slept with.
The Psychiatric Unit white with snow.
The red-haired nurse spent all day in the day-room
although she was off-duty.
How do you know?
Enormous jerseys and no knickers. Sand.
Crystallized rose-petals. Ashes. Sheep.
We watched the moorhens treading through the tree-tops,
their big green feet like camels'.
Itchy skin.

Is she quiet and listless all the time,
or is there something I should do, she wondered.
Sitting looking utterly defeated,
fingering the books she's not allowed.
The bullfinches, the bats, the precious letters
gobbled up for nothing.
Go away.

The same good-looking man who liked my cardigan.
Or is that just my illness?
Fairy cakes.
The shaggy remains of a star give sweet instruction
to sleepless lovers.
"What does he mean – he's *'going'*?"
I want to scream and scream and all I do
is write *I want to scream* down in my book.
Fathers coming closer like the tide.
One word.
Enclosed by hate.
I feel like string.
Apricots. Gold. Massed ascensions. Jam.
They're coming now. They're going to flood my veins.

The patients rise like early morning milk.

The planets' movements alternate the tides.
The waiting-room. It frightens me. The hole.
DISEASES OF THE MIND. Pet monkeys. Silk.

Wild bees know little joy.
No visitors.
I've wanted to go home all my life.
Moving deeper into purple woodland.
Lop-eared rabbits, walnuts. Wearing boots.
Ginger weasels cross the gated road.
The little dog is limping.
So am I.
My mother says I'm hopeless.
Bits of lettuce.
The doctor wrote it down:
'Her haunted mind.'

He buttoned up the collar of my jacket
and whispered in my ear 'She's dying now.'
Boiled ham and tulips.
It was evening.
I never want to help you.
"Say Goodbye."

"I like the way you're breathless – it's erotic."
People who leave London will be shot.
Antibiotics. Sleet. My 'fortitude'.
That blissful state in which you feel forgotten.
To get a little carpet in our bedroom,
to go under the door, a little planed.
Afternoons of fruit and acts of kindness.
"Is it true you're not allowed a mirror?"
Your mother called and said she left your washing
crying on the disinfected floor.
A lovely lady's holding out a rabbit.
The lady smiles. The rabbit's name is Pam.
My skirt is like a lorry full of whiskers.
It makes me feel sick to think of him.

The nurse has got a rabbit. Yes, it's mine!
I love its gleaming harmony!
Apologies,
I *used* to have a rabbit I called Pam.

Voices I keep catching all the time.
A mohair cardigan. A bowl of pears.
I know she said don't listen to the voices.
I've been depressed for over twenty years.

All the baby's family are missing.
Espadrilles. Potatoes. Women saints.
Her carrycot is floating in the sea.
It's 4 o'clock. The rabbit's wide awake.
"People say it's all so free and honest."
The walls are green. "He said, 'You're schizophrenic!'"
The feeling of the nurses' hands. I'm blind.
No time for sorrow's rippling fish. I'm blood-soaked.
The corner of the day-room shines like coal.
Soon I will be better. At the moment
I live in humble darkness like the mole.

The gravel drive makes everybody stumble.
The Virgin in her wooden dress is kind.
Red roses tumble softly onto water.
The day-room smells of toffee. I don't mind.

"Loving me is not enough." He laughed,
feeling with his fingers up my skirt.
He looked into my frightened, rubber eye-balls.
He smelt of fennel, weasels, sandy dirt.

Inmates waltz at dusk at party-time.
Sitting by herself in fairyland.
"It's far too late to start remembering now!"
The smell of fennel when they move. Thick tea.
The sun is setting. It is time to start.
"Everyone admires our Christmas Tree!"

Sausages and chips and apple crumble.

Everything she does is always wrong.
The vicar gave us lovely cards and honey.
The rich girl says her father won't be long.

Moving hands and horses fill the sky.
I do not need a coat. *Leave me alone.*
The red-eyed doctors block the corridors
with turquoise needles tipped with Methadone.

The rocks like leopards soften in the rain.
I see myself as Jesus' private nun,
lost in the mists of time, when we were little –
mushrooms; herons; woolly bears; my mum.

I had to cross the day-room on my hands,
a silent rabbit foraging for fruit.
I dread the human voice. The doctor said
"There's nothing we can do. We need your bed."

The doctor's squirting juice into my eyes.
Her name is Pam.
"I didn't say a thing."
A bowl of cornflakes feels a shower of sugar;
the erotic zone of Sister feels the same.

I think I have swallowed a rabbit.
It keeps wriggling.
Reflections in still water.
"Is that right?"

Someone has painted my movements. I am banned.
As thick as purple gravy when I strain.
The porter eats his dinner with his hands.
I saw him eating in my bed again.

The daily wards of underwater fame.
Swimming to the pills.
Don't say my name.

The hospital is underwater, Trixie.
To widen brains, please nail all joints loosely.

This little thing's been homeless for so long.
Now say goodbye.
She won't be very long.

PART TWO
The Out-Patient

CHAPTER 1 Masters

I step across the white dust of the runway
towards a man with pistols for a face.
He's tall and thin with one hand in a bandage.
I hear a faint pow-pow of disgrace.

'Departing for womanhood.' Crap. Green velvet cushions.
The baker's sons are being introduced.
The canteen of the airport smells of pepper.
I follow him towards the setting sun.
The avenue of cacti like an elephant
shelter silent groups of staring men.
We go upstairs. His buckle scrapes the brick-work.
Lust and grief. Unusual cakes. He's kind.
I'm menstruating on a stranger's blankets.
Sorrow like a silver spool unwinds.

The sun is hot. My head is full of silence
attracting hordes of angry bees like bells.
A swallow-tail, an amber necklace, henna.
I want to be so calm. 'Devotion frees.'

People, horizontal, lit, ascending,
now declare their everlasting love
by open windows, where the tepid evening
is tempting them to cast aside their clothes.

Unfriendly geese stand by the fence like nurses,
and sheep run down the fluffy hill in rows.

See me see me see me in the garden.
I'm made of ants.
Whose voice is that?
It's hers.
Feel between my legs two lips like lollies,
or like a blood-hound on the verge of tears.

Talking to him in a voice as distant
as unborn daughters kneeling by my bed.

Turkish delight, brazil nuts, sweetened yoghurt.
I treasure every word I think he said.

The only men were doctors. We were dollies
put to sleep in resonating halls.

The bell is ringing like an English cherry.
Picasso in his villa touches girls.

The boots that crush the roses hear me whisper
You mustn't kiss me now. He takes my hand.
Ecstasy, which makes him feel nearer,
has made me ill. I never talk. I'm banned.

The offices are empty, only you:
a violet light, a pleated skirt, a prayer
rising in the dark then drifting downward
to join the other voices of the air;
while in the muted villa, calmed by sorrow,
someone feels a lightening of snow.
We'll move you to another bed tomorrow,
we'll move you to a place where good girls go.

CHAPTER 2 Strangers

Bluebells, Bovril, somebody's blind spaniel.
The bluebells shine with Daddy's violet light.

She even brought her mole with her. *Don't cry.*
She ran about the rocks till it was night.

Toast and cream. Her deep-blue velvet dresses.
I haven't told the others where I've been.

Dragonflies fly round her head in traces.
There may be someone there – we'll have to see.

Someone to talk to, cold as charity.
An analgesic and a febrifuge.

Lop-eared sheep in echoing ravines.
The tiny nun is venturing to intrude.

Lamented daughters slip away like cats;
running water; seals; grace abounding:

a crippled Coptic mother's early sorrows,
through centuries of beaten earth resounding.

The doctors say my shyness is repellent.
The shyness of the bittern. I'm alone,

living in a world where pinks and pumas
drink cherry-flavoured drops of Methadone.

The other people cut down all the trees
and vivisect the cats and toads. *Roulette.*

Making honey sandwiches. Misgivings.
The way my mother handles ducks. *Nanette.*

Even the Central Predigstuhl's West Gully
denied us shelter in its icy palace.

Irish monks in frail craft made of leather
discovered Iceland, glaciers and solace.

The golden dribbles of the butterscotch
tremble on the rubber. She can't swim.

She's singing like a lover through the water,
singing through the glass her blue-green hymn.

Crystal quartz like love from Colorado.
Sealed with rheum. The chickens' sunlit meal

scattered on the lily-pond. *'Raw, tender,
hostile, hot or bored – how do you feel?'*

I feel like a table-cloth with grazing rights;
a newt; a guinea-fowl; a tulip-head;

the listlessness of rivers' eels; bandages.
Don't tell me what you think I should have said!

My body's like a zebra's; rock-hard plums;
the glittering of quartz washed by the sea;

Dorothy Wordsworth's toothache, like a crystal;
THE WONDERFUL WORLD OF HORSES; amber tea.

Measuring my sleeping lover's neck.
Chicken thighs. A greeting. *Take your time.*

Running water soothes; a little music.
I can't imagine what it's like. *Like mine.*

His hand is lying on my lap like liver.
Wiping up the blood. He's very kind.

Every little star must twinkle brighter.
The poor thing's got no breasts. *O never mind.*

Bunches of butchered seagulls. Dusky archers.
You must be someone special. *Hold my hand.*

Bit by bit, not suddenly. Peach. Barley.
I thought you were never coming. *Hold my hand.*

The handsome sleeping generals lie massacred
like beautiful white flour from Singapore.

34

Who but a beaten specialist would offer
to map the changes of the ocean floor?

I didn't say a word about the therapy.
The doctors deal in glitter-coated worms.

A schizophrenic dressed in silk to please him,
I part my lips like lilac, brush his sperm.

I said I was afraid of him, and everyone.
My mother was a copper kangaroo.

Liquorice and shrimps inside her locker.
I go to pieces in the afternoon.

I think the nurse said she was going to shoot me.
I can't sit up. I don't know what to say.

The bead-like packing may be tiny pearls. *Hush*,
everyone loves fear. Don't go away.

The shaved and beaded Maasai mothers calmly
wash their sons in milk from special cows.

He said that if I walk along serenely,
I'm worthy of their gold and violet flowers.

They broke into my room, and I was murdered –
innocent, illuminated, rose.

I cannot touch my cup in case they see me.
My mother leaves my laundry with the nurse.

She turns the light out, leaving me in darkness,
a dumb, adored, impassive amulet:

ah, I will be so lovely in the summertime,
when Doctor parts my sleepy body's net.

The central point round which the volumes settle,
his doll is staring like the smell of gas.

He wants to be alone with me. I'm sweating.
My body will dissolve. "Can't you relax?"

A dress-maker of hollyhocks and butter,
lying headless on my sunlit porch,

waiting by the door to see the doctor –
hear me play my isolated chords!

Sunny days of quiet desperation.
"She misses her poor daughter still, you know."

Sunlight. Netball. Ankle-socks. White rabbits.
Ceaseless prayer like purity of snow.

Rescued from her introverted nightmare
by seeing washing billowing on the line.

Doing certain things. "Yes, please sit anywhere!"
We sit on any surface we can find.

'Write a list of gratifying activities.'
Tomato juice makes glasses hard to clean.

Suddenly the man leans down and bites me.
The lily-pond – the carp – the bluebells' gleam.

The gods of Europe shower me with smiles,
unnerving all the men that come and stare;

I dance until my heart begins to break –
then Sister comes and makes me brush my hair.

The dog has got a little curly tail
the size and texture of a tangerine.

The bluebells are as glossy as the horses,
galloping like lust into the sea.

The penned imported camels by the villa,
like ghostly castles made of sand and bone,

lean their narrow hips against the darkness,
waiting for a love they've never known.

CHAPTER 3 Monks

I am alone. Where are they? Snowy weather.
Am I allowed to write like this or not?
She said that I could go to the meeting,
and then she said that I had better not.

The girl in my room is reading ALONE WITH OTHERS.
I really feel I can't go through with this.
'Walking through a forest with a parcel.'
And all she wants is my companionship.

Chicory, cashew nuts, paper zebras.
"Why do you look so worried?" I don't know.
The voices fade. The floor is piled with cushions.
I wonder, will she speak when we're alone?

We are the children of This. This is the silence.
I haven't talked to anyone for days.
I can hear a pony's rhythmic cropping.
I can feel the wind against my face.

"It's been a lovely friendly convalescence,
and I shall go home feeling much much better . . ."
It's miles getting back . . . but we don't care . . .
miles and miles . . . it really doesn't matter.

Larches in the forest bring the evening.
Disabled men drink milk among fat hens.
A sense of loss like violins pursues me
and will not let me sleep, the young man says.

Piano Pieces, fruit, embroidered slippers.
Struggle for what? Eurhythmy. Green and neat,
scentless mayweed, dragonflies, tall grasses
ripple in the grounds like greyhounds' feet.

The man who dances like the sea surrounds me.
I'm shivering. I'm sorry. It's so new.
The Spiritual Head of the Order's started laughing.

Piles of strawberry jam. "May I laugh too?"

As blossom fills the lawns of scented gardens,
fluttering whispers fill the patient's throat.
Love is more than simple acts of kindness:
it comes from deep within us like a note.

They play the flute until it's nearly morning.
The man who heals with sound is by my side.
My meditation's swilled with icy water
for Ahto and Vellamo, Ahto's bride.

Horses pass unseen in the forest,
a speckled bantam suddenly takes flight;
Molly, who is over eighty, 's mending
the wooden boat she painted gold last night.

"What does he mean by meditation anyway?"
She looks so lonely with her little plaits.
Secret letters. Failing to adore him.
Invisible vanilla. Roses. Cats.

The dogs are neither elegant nor handsome,
but make us feel warm when we are cold.
The sleeping monks are sailing into morning;
soya milk like cowries; silence; gold.

Tinned faces. Yellow cushions. *Love him more.*
And let your body say what you can't say.
It's just a little shower, she said, her suffering.
It's nice to know you like me. "It's O.K."

The stone floor cools the dogs and the chicory,
the memories of H., demented, dim;
the heat-wave is receding from the flowers
piled in her basket like the wind.

She said that I could join the group tomorrow,
her tilted pools of everlasting wealth!
Someone in my dream is always smiling.
'You think it must be God but it's yourself.'

Community of nuns in Andalusia.
Colossal love like thunder. Bowls of shells.
The dancer had a giant dog called Hilda
who used to like to eat the daffodils.

The patient from the villa came to visit.
Rabbit fur, damp leaves. She didn't stay.
The Sister has retired to the country –
irises and blackbirds, flowering may.

Like mottled soap of olive-oil and soda;
Nivea; flat stones, their edges gone;
the soles of people paddling in the tide-line,
I feel I am being acted on.

Gardening gloves touch pale blue hydrangeas;
'becoming aware of myself as something known';
my dog has gone to sleep across my pillow;
'keep the mind in the middle of the tongue.'

The hooded men who follow me and whisper
have slipped away like weasels in the snow.
I too must say good-bye to the monastery.
The train is waiting. "Really, I must go!"

PART THREE
The Last Week

Friday

And all the time,
the heifers' solemn faces
are breathing by my side,
as soft as ash;
my little fire
is burning in the moonlight
that slips between the grasses
like a cat.

Saturday

The painted bows.
The silver nail-scissors.
Strips of paper in a stencilled tin.
A flannel in a bowl.
Hush. What's the matter?
Early morning sunlight, paper-thin.

My breath is like the long electric hair
of someone swinging on a high trapeze:
it sweeps the air and all the faces cry
ha; and again *ha!*
What turns you on?

Sunday

The river-bank is thick with summer flowers,
as stiff as pigs, as pink as fruit; massed flies
stroke their wings against the fluted sky
whose height, as sweet as hay, rings like an axe
and dyes the spotted cows a million blues.

Monday

At midnight we have rolls and oranges.
My hands are cold.
They make me cups of tea.
Sons and daughters, singing in the moonlight,
are drifting on their tin beds out to sea.

Ankle-bones,
peach-slices,
mignonette;
bars of chocolate,
fur:
I won't forget.

Tuesday

I'm sitting on my blanket
eating toast.
In India I starved.
I'm very fat.
Mother Teresa, Mother Teresa calling.
She wants me now.
She wants me in her flat.

A stream of sons
in striped pyjamas lies
listening to the chanting
rise like bees
from buzzing hives
to heaven's lighted windows,
as morning breaks,
and cows approach the yard.

Wednesday

A lame man walks for miles along a beach;
the dazzling sunlight magnifies his dreams:
a pool of blood that soaks into the pine-woods,
a bungalow, dead rabbits, skin-tight jeans.

Thursday

The afternoon
is giving way
to evening,
I help my tearful daughter
rinse her hair;
a bullfinch
in the holm oak
calmly singing;
my holiday;
Nijinsky;
ginger air.

From grassy hills
and dark pink trees
come hopping
frogs and crickets
into beams of light.
The air beside my bed's
a ballerina
dancing in the arches of the night.

My sleeping-bag smells sweetly
of the pine-wood,
my smoky hair and pillows
of warm stones.
The terns fly off like splinters of the evening.
I'm glad there's no-one here.
Peach-slices.
Bones.

Friday

My sister has been racing someone's race-horse
across a valley in the pouring rain,
trying to forgive
our blood-stained mother
who killed her German Shepherd,
Violet.

The Minuet for Berenice is playing;
everything seems normal, but it's not:
we look as if we're drawing, but we're praying,
our studio of birds, our brotherhood.

Instant mashed potato, lettuce, Spam.
The rabbit on the plate is going shopping.
The islands of potato warm the lettuce
and stir the little virgin jockey's heart.

The Boyle Family. Walsingham. Hot water.
"She hasn't left her drawing-board all day."
The warm dog and the Little Tern run quietly
to Everlasting Light on polished toes.

Saturday

Your voice is clear as crystal,
so is mine;
as turquoise,
divers,
steel,
turpentine.
Your fingers smell of Nivea,
it's cold,
your fingers smell of pine-woods and the sky;
you touch my hands,
you wash my eyes in water
enclosed in heated towels. *Say good-bye.*

'Every sort of pine will yield resin
for incense, violins and ballet-shoes.
The creamy tears are found in natural fissures,
or trickling from the wounds of broken boughs.'

The boats are on the grass,
the sun is shining,
the station-master tends his flower-bed.
I feel I am dancing underwater
and Christ is by my side, the dancer said.